Saving Endangered Species

by
Catherine Podojil

Editorial Offices: Glenview, Illinois • Parsippany, New Jersey • New York, New York
Sales Offices: Needham, Massachusetts • Duluth, Georgia • Glenview, Illinois
Coppell, Texas • Ontario, California • Mesa, Arizona

Every effort has been made to secure permission and provide appropriate credit for photographic material. The publisher deeply regrets any omission and pledges to correct errors called to its attention in subsequent editions.

Unless otherwise acknowledged, all photographs are the property of Scott Foresman, a division of Pearson Education.

Photo locators denoted as follows: Top (T), Center (C), Bottom (B), Left (L), Right (R), Background (Bkgd)

Opener: Brand X Pictures; 1 Brand X Pictures; 3 (B) Brand X Pictures; 4 (C) Digital Vision, (BC) Getty Images; 5 (BL, BR) Getty Images; 6 ©DK Images; 7 (BL) Sullivan & Rogers/Bruce Coleman Inc., (C) Getty Images; 8 (CL) Getty Images, (B) Digital Stock; 9 (B) Digital Vision, (CR) Getty Images; 10 Digital Vision; 11 Getty Images; 12 Digital Vision; 13 Photo Researchers, Inc.; 14 (C, B) Digital Vision; 15 Getty Images; 16 Getty Images; 17 (BL, C) Getty Images; 18–19 Toyohiro Yamada/Getty Images; 20 (CL) Digital Stock, (B) Flat Earth; 21 (BR) Digital Vision; 22 (BL) Brand X Pictures, (BR) Getty Images

ISBN: 0-328-13528-3

Copyright © Pearson Education, Inc.

All Rights Reserved. Printed in the United States of America. This publication is protected by Copyright, and permission should be obtained from the publisher prior to any prohibited reproduction, storage in a retrieval system, or transmission in any form by any means, electronic, mechanical, photocopying, recording, or likewise. For information regarding permission(s), write to: Permissions Department, Scott Foresman, 1900 East Lake Avenue, Glenview, Illinois 60025.

4 5 6 7 8 9 10 V0G1 14 13 12 11 10 09 08 07 06

Why do species become extinct?

Over time many types, or **species,** of animals and plants have become **extinct.** When a species becomes extinct, none of its kind ever exist again. This happens for many reasons. For example, two animal species may eat the same food, but if one species is a better hunter and can find more food, then the other species may not get enough food to survive. Also, some animals survive by eating only one kind of food, and as a result can die off if that food source suddenly becomes scarce. This means that a dramatic change in climate that killed a species of plant would also kill the animal species that ate only that plant.

You may have heard the theory that many scientists have about how the dinosaurs became extinct. About 65 million years ago, a giant asteroid hit Earth, sending tons of dust and rock flying into the air and blocking out some of the Sun's rays. Many scientists believe that without enough energy from the Sun, plants everywhere died. The dinosaurs that depended on those plants for food all died because they had no more to eat, and without plant eaters, the meat-eating dinosaurs also became extinct.

Dinosaur extinction was caused by natural events.

Extinction Today

According to the latest calculations by scientists, upwards of forty thousand species of plants and animals are now becoming extinct each year. It's hard to imagine forty thousand kinds of mammals, birds, amphibians, reptiles, insects, flowers, and trees disappearing forever! Many of these species do not become extinct because of natural events; rather, they become extinct because of human actions.

People cut down forests to build homes, roads, businesses, and farms. In this way many species of animals and plants lose their homes, or **habitats.** The loss of an animal's habitat can lead to extinction. Humans also destroy habitats by polluting the land, water, and air, which are also called environments. Furthermore, the chemicals and plants that we use can hurt plants and animals. As the number of humans grows, we use more land and make more pollution, driving more and more species to extinction.

Logging (far left), pollution (middle), and drilling for oil (below) all cause habitat loss.

A Lesson Learned

In the 1800s there were billions of passenger pigeons in North America. They flew in flocks of millions that were up to three hundred miles long! The speed at which the passenger pigeons flew, estimated at sixty miles an hour, was also amazing. The birds migrated from Canada to areas in the southeastern United States, including parts of Texas, Louisiana, Alabama, Georgia, and Florida.

In Wayne County, New York, a local resident described passenger pigeons in flight by saying, "There would be days and days when the air was alive with them . . . Flocks stretched as far as a person could see. . . ." No one could imagine the passenger pigeon becoming extinct.

But that is exactly what happened. The passenger pigeon ate mostly nuts from beech and oak trees. In the 1800s huge oak and beech forests were cut down for fuel and lumber. Hunters also killed millions of the birds for food and to sell.

Conservationists tried to stop the overhunting, but people ignored the laws. The few pigeons left were put into a breeding program, but this failed because the remaining **population** was too small to breed successfully. Martha, the last passenger pigeon on Earth, died in 1914 at the Cincinnati Zoo.

The passenger pigeon was probably the most common bird in the world. Now there isn't a single one anywhere on Earth.

What can people do?

During the late twentieth century, people became worried by the fact that so many species were in danger of becoming extinct. Conservationists began to call for protections to preserve species that were at risk. In response, in 1973, the U.S. Congress passed the Endangered Species Act. This act protects certain animals and plants from hunting, collecting, and other harmful activities.

Two kinds of species are protected under the act. **Endangered** species are those that scientists believe will become extinct within twenty years if they are not protected. Among the most well-known endangered species are the California condor, the cheetah, the snow leopard, the Bengal tiger, the manatee, and the blue whale.

The snow leopard, which lives in the mountains of Asia, is endangered.

The other protected species are called **threatened.** Threatened species are those that are not yet endangered but are at risk of becoming endangered. Since the Endangered Species Act was passed, the status of some species has improved enough to allow them to be upgraded from endangered to threatened. Populations of peregrine falcons, bald eagles, and American alligators have all increased enough that they are no longer in great danger of extinction. However, these species still need to be watched to ensure their survival, and because of that they are considered threatened.

The bald eagle, a symbol of freedom in the United States, is threatened.

Saving the Condor

Sometimes it is possible to bring back a species that is almost extinct. The California condor, for example, had almost completely disappeared from the wild by the 1980s. Today, their numbers are rising, thanks to some very hardworking people.

The California condor is one of the largest flying birds on Earth. Adult condors can have wingspans of nine feet and weigh up to twenty-five pounds. Their feathers are mostly black, except for a patch of white under each wing. Condors' feathers cover their entire bodies, with the exception of their heads, which are pinkish orange in color. Condors once lived all over North America, but habitat loss has pushed them into isolated areas in parts of western Canada, the United States, and Mexico.

The California condor is a **scavenger,** meaning that it eats dead animals instead of hunting live ones. It glides high above the ground, floating on updrafts of warm air, and finds food with its powerful eyes. California condors can glide at more than fifty miles per hour and will fly more than one hundred miles a day looking for food.

The California condor is one of the largest flying birds on Earth.

The number of California condors shrank during the 1900s. Chemicals used to kill insects made the birds' eggshells too thin, preventing them from hatching correctly. Farmers and hunters killed many condors inadvertently, by poisoning coyotes and other animals. When the condors ate these dead animals, the poison also killed them. By 1985 there were only nine California condors left in the wild.

Realizing how perilous the situation was, the government captured the remaining nine wild condors. Scientists hoped to breed them and release their offspring into the wild. This is harder than it sounds, since condors reproduce very slowly. In the wild, female condors lay eggs at a rate of only one every other year, but scientists came up with a way to trick the birds into laying more eggs. The trick they used involved taking the condor's egg out of the nest as soon as it was laid, causing the female bird to lay another egg right away. The young condors that hatched from the extra eggs were fed by scientists who wore condor hand puppets to fool the young condors into thinking that they were being fed by their mothers.

Condor puppets are used to keep the baby condors from becoming dependent on their human caretakers.

The breeding program has been extremely successful. In 1992 the first condors were released in southern California, and more have since been released in Arizona. Not all of them lived. Some were killed by people, some could not adapt to the wild, and some had become too dependent on humans.

In 2002 the first condor egg was laid in the wild. As of April 2004, there were ninety-four California condors living in the wild. They nest in California, Arizona, and Mexico. Others are being bred and held for release. Now some condor chicks are raised by adult condors instead of people. The condor breeding program is a conservation success!

A baby condor right after hatching from its egg.

The Andean Condor

An even larger endangered condor, the Andean condor, lives in the Andes mountains of South America. This huge bird's ten-foot wingspan makes it slightly bigger than its California cousin. It also has a "collar" of white feathers around its lower neck.

Fortunately, programs have been put in place to help save the Andean condor. A group in Argentina raises condor chicks in a zoo and then returns them to the wild. People keep track of the newly released adults by using satellites. The satellite tracking has shown that the birds fly over a much larger area than people once thought. As a result, South America's national parks are now thought to be too small to protect the Andean condor. So conservationists are teaching South American people about the value of the condor and why it needs to be protected.

What about habitats?

As you read earlier, many species become extinct when they lose their habitats. Raising animals in breeding programs so they can be released into the wild is important, but those animals still need a home to live in once they've been let back out! Because of that, people have come to see that saving animals' habitats is as important as saving animals.

One animal that desperately needs to have its habitat saved is the grizzly bear. The grizzly bear is one of the largest animals in North America. Male grizzly bears can stand on their hind legs to a height of seven feet!

You've probably heard stories of grizzlies attacking hikers. In fact, such incidents happen very rarely, and many more people are attacked by domestic animals such as dogs. But humans should be watchful when they are in the wilderness. Food that is not locked up will attract grizzlies, as well as other animals. It's also important to act in ways that will not frighten grizzly cubs. Grizzly mothers will attack if they think their cubs are in danger.

The grizzly bear is one of the largest land animals in North America.

Grizzlies need huge amounts of land to live well and thrive. Each grizzly's habitat may take up as many as five hundred square miles! At one time the grizzly lived all over Canada, the western United States, and parts of Mexico, but by the 1970s it had lost 98 percent of its original habitat.

Today, grizzly bears live in the U.S. and Canadian Rocky Mountains and in Alaska. They also live in Yellowstone National Park. Groups are working to connect grizzlies' Canadian and U.S. habitats, to give them more room to move around.

There are several threats to the grizzly bear. Building roads through forests destroys the grizzly's habitat. Many bears are also killed on these roads. Bears eat everything, from nuts and berries to elk and even the garbage that we create. This can cause problems. Eating trash puts grizzlies close to humans, which can be dangerous for all involved.

By the 1970s the grizzly bear had lost 98 percent of its original habitat.

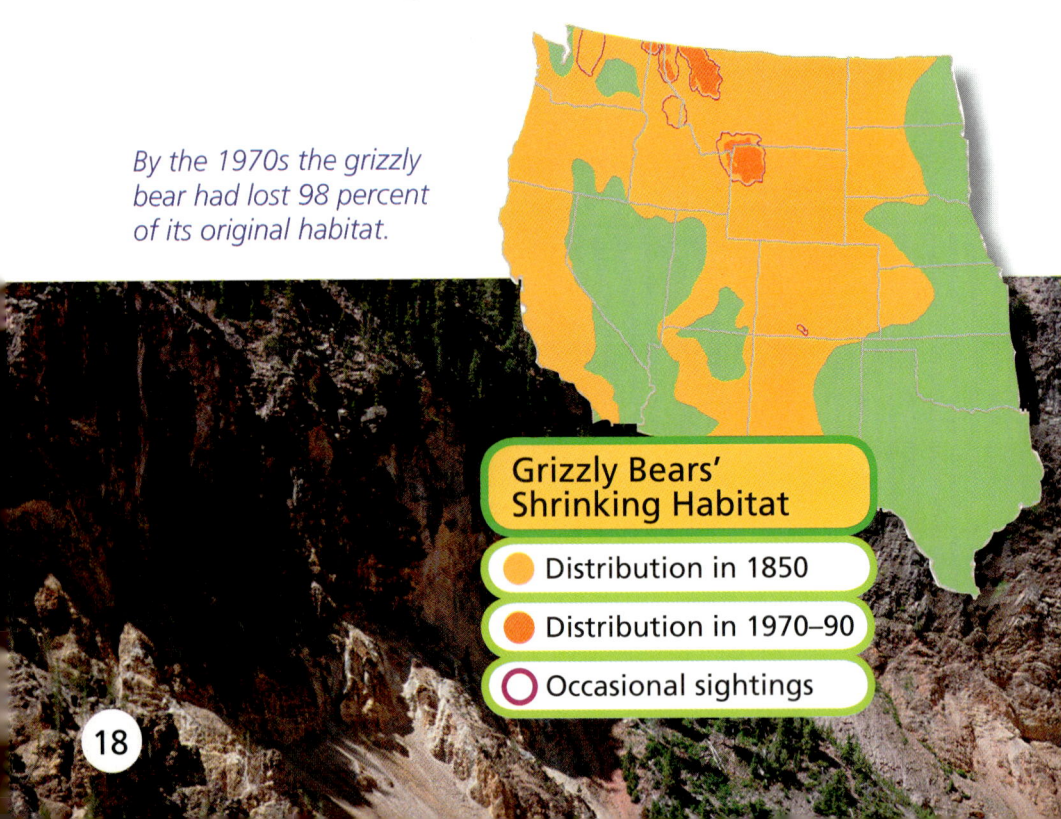

Grizzly Bears' Shrinking Habitat

● Distribution in 1850
● Distribution in 1970–90
○ Occasional sightings

Wildlife groups work to resolve these issues. They have learned that elk and bears need similar habitats. As a result, people who like to hunt elk have gotten involved with protecting grizzlies' habitats. Some groups have tried to keep logging companies from building more roads in forests, but it is not an easy task. Also, people work to ensure that the grizzly stays on the endangered list. If it is "de-listed," or removed, it will no longer be protected.

Elk are not the only animals that thrive in a grizzly's habitat. Keeping a habitat healthy for bears also keeps trout and salmon swimming in the streams and birds nesting in the trees. These connections help people see the forest in a different way. Once, they may have seen it only as a source of timber or a place to build houses. Now, with education about endangered animals, they see it as a place for many species to live. But the struggle is hard. Without help from the government and conservation groups, the little that remains of the grizzly's habitat could soon disappear.

Habitats that are good for grizzly bears are good for many other animals as well.

Other Countries, Other Rescues

As you have read, the United States is not the only country where animals and plants are in danger. Tigers are in trouble in Asian countries, and elephants are endangered in Asia and threatened in Africa. Sea mammals, such as manatees, are threatened by fishing, pollution, and ships, and saltwater crocodiles were almost wiped out in Australia before steps were taken to protect them.

In India the Wild Lands Elephant Corridor Project is working to protect elephants and other animals. These corridors are actually strips of land that allow elephants to move around the country without being bothered by humans. The elephants can move from one protected area to another along pathways that protect them from poaching and other harm.

In India, people are working to protect the Asian elephant.

In Cambodia, people are trying to save the tiger. People hunt tigers illegally for their skin, teeth, and other parts. These illegal hunters, or poachers, earn a lot of money by hunting tigers. New programs pay these poachers to protect the tigers instead. In this way the poachers become conservationists and work to save tigers.

Wildlife and wildlife habitats are popular tourist attractions in many countries. People enjoy getting close to wildlife and learning about different animal species. They appreciate their beauty and begin to think more about the need to protect them.

Humans share the Earth with many other living things. As our population grows, our need for food and energy increases. We take up more and more room, which leaves less room for plants and animals. People must learn new and better ways of finding and using resources. If we don't, some of nature's most beautiful and amazing creatures will disappear forever.

Tigers are in danger of becoming extinct.

Now Try This

Endangered Species Report

Look up some endangered or threatened species. Choose one that interests you. You may choose a species from your area or from far away. If you're from the southern United States, you might choose the manatee. If you're from a northern state, you might choose the gray wolf. If you live near a desert area, you might choose the desert tortoise. Or you may choose a species that does not live in your country, such as the snow leopard or the African elephant.

Collect information from books or the Internet about your endangered species. What is being done to save it? How successful have these efforts been? Is there anything you could do to help save this animal?

Here's How to Do It!

Write and illustrate a report on your species. Include a description of what the animal looks like, what it eats, and what kind of habitat it needs. Then tell why the species is in danger. Is your animal's habitat being destroyed by people? Is its food becoming scarce? Is the animal hunted for its skin or other body parts? Include these kinds of details in your report. Finally, tell what is being done to rescue the animal from extinction and your ideas for what can be done in the future.

Illustrate your book with your own drawings, pictures from the Internet, or both. Find pictures of the animal and its habitat and write captions to describe each picture. Then design a cover for your report so that it looks like a book. Once your report is complete, share it with the class.

Glossary

conservationists *n.* people who work to preserve and protect forests, rivers, plant and animal species, and other natural resources.

endangered *adj.* in danger of becoming extinct.

extinct *adj.* no longer existing.

habitats *n.* places where animals or plants live or grow naturally.

population *n.* all the living things of one kind in a single place.

scavenger *n.* a living thing that eats dead animal matter.

species *n.* a group of organisms that have common traits and can breed with each other.

threatened *adj.* at risk of becoming endangered.